Epitaphs in Red: Poems of The Damned

By K.W. Krieger

A Grim Advisory (Not That It'll Help)

Dearest Reader,

You've opened a book that smells faintly of regret, despair, and perhaps a hint of mildew. Congratulations. Within these pages lies a collection of tales and verses steeped in darkness, painted in blood, and embroidered with the tears of the foolishly curious—people much like yourself.

Let's set the record straight: this is not a book of pleasant rhymes or uplifting stanzas. No, this is a literary mausoleum, a cemetery of words where each poem serves as an epitaph for the lost, the damned, and the terminally unlucky.

This book will trigger you. Yes, you. The sensitive, the stoic, the skeptic, and the unflinchingly brave—no one leaves unscathed. These pages do not "explore" darkness; they wallow in it, revel in it, and drag you down with them. It's not a suggestion that you might be disturbed—it's a promise.

Here's your warning: expect themes of death, betrayal, madness, grotesque violence, suicide, and horrors that stretch beyond the veil of human comprehension. Don't worry about whether this book is "too much" for you—it absolutely is. If your first instinct is to clutch your pearls or cry out for a therapist, stop now and find a book club where they discuss tepid romances or inspirational quotes. This one's not for you, sweetheart.

For those of you who thrive on the macabre, welcome to the dark carnival. But let's get one thing straight: this book doesn't love you. It won't hold your hand or whisper reassuring platitudes in your ear. It will shove you into the abyss, kick you while you're down, and laugh while you claw at the edge.

The ink on these pages is still wet with misery, and the shadows between the lines might bite. These poems won't just tell you stories;

they'll reach into your soul, leave muddy footprints on your sanity, and invite the nightmares to stay awhile.

You thought these words were safe to read, but now they root, planting seeds of doubt and dread. Each line you've read has whispered to the darkness just beyond your vision, and it's listening. The book you clutch will hum with malice when you turn the final page, and when you shut it—oh, don't think you've escaped.

Now, if you're still clutching this collection with trembling hands and morbid anticipation, I can only assume you're either a glutton for punishment or someone who enjoys whispering into the void to see if it whispers back. Either way, you're already damned, so you might as well keep reading.

Enjoy, if that's even the right word.
(And don't say we didn't warn you.)

With dubious sincerity and blood-soaked disdain,
The Author
(Or the thing hiding under your bed tonight)

Epitaph Index

Epitaphs in Red

Beneath the moon's unyielding glow,
Where shadows stretch and horrors grow,
The pages lie, their verses cursed,
A dirge for souls the night has nursed.

This book, a tome of tales untold,
In scarlet ink, the stories unfold.
Each line a wound, each stanza a scar,
A monument to those who are.

No hymn of joy, no light divine,
These words are etched in sorrow's line.
For in these lines, the living tread,
Through whispers of the restless dead.

A poet's blade, a quill's sharp edge,
Cuts deeper than a solemn pledge.
Each stroke a life, each phrase a cry,
A final breath, a soft goodbye.

The hunter's lair, the maiden's plea,
The ghostly wail beneath the sea.

The forest dark, the watcher's grin,
The sins we hide, the monsters within.

Turn not too quick, nor read too light,
These verses haunt the edge of night.
They call to those who dare to see,
The cost of life, the end's decree.

Yet through the dread, a beauty blooms,
A crimson rose in shadowed rooms.
For death itself can be sublime,
A fleeting truth, unbound by time.

So open wide this sanguine book,
And take the risk, the fateful look.
For every tale, a truth is bled,
In these, our **Epitaphs in Red**.

Blood and Ink

Beneath the pale and flickering light,
The writer toils through endless night.
A quill in hand, a heart laid bare,
Yet shadows whisper everywhere.

The ink, it flows, a river black,
From parchment's edge, there's no way back.
Each word a scar, each line a plea,
A tale of anguish, bound to be.

But in the ink, a crimson thread,
A darker hue where life has bled.
The pen, it cuts, the pages tear,
As blood and ink entwine despair.

The room grows cold, the air turns thin,
As something stirs beneath the skin.
The verses writhe, the letters crawl,
A summoning, beyond the scrawl.

The quill now moves with ghostly grace,
No hand to guide, no time, no place.

Its strokes grow sharp, the pages weep,
A pact of flesh that death will keep.

At dawn, the writer fades from view,
The words remain, the ink's dark hue.
A tale of pain, a cursed brink—
Forever bound in blood and ink.

Whispered Blade

Beneath the moon's unholy stare,
In shadows deep, a hunter's lair,
A heart beats loud, yet none will hear,
The creeping tread of death so near.

The forest hums a mournful tune,
A hymn to match the waning moon.
The boughs above, they twist and writhe,
As silent steel begins to thrive.

A breath, a gasp—a fleeting life,
The crimson bloom of butchered strife.
Eyes wide with shock, no time for prayer,
For mercy fled the midnight air.

The blade, it dances, sharp and lean,
Its wicked edge a glint unseen.
A ghostly whisper seals the fate,
Of souls who linger, far too late.

No heroes come to save the night,
Just endless dark and fading light.
And in the wake, the earth will keep,
The secrets of the ones who sleep.

So tread with care, where shadows glide,
For murder walks, and will not hide.

Eyes of the Void

The stars do not blink.
They see you beneath their gaze.
Run—they've chosen you.

Crimson Pact

The clock struck twelve, the hour grim,
When shadows danced on a moonlight whim.
A house stood still, its breath held tight,
A tomb for dreams devoured by night.

Upon the floor, a scarlet thread,
It weaved a tale the silence fed.
Each drop of red, a whispered cry,
Each stain a vow that none deny.

The dagger gleamed, a viper's smile,
Its thirst unquenched, its charm beguile.
In trembling hands, its purpose clear,
To draw the truth from flesh and fear.

She called him close, her voice a sigh,
"A bond of blood, we can't untie."
He stepped too near, her eyes like flame,
Too late, he learned her wicked game.

A lunge, a scream, a final breath,
The room grew cold with sudden death.
Yet on her lips, a tender grin,
For sin had called—and she let sin in.

And as the clock resumed its pace,
No trace remained of time's embrace.
But echoes roamed where murder played,
A haunting hymn that never fades.

The Room

The door is locked tight,
The walls whisper with no voice—
You cannot escape.

The Hollow Guest

The night was thick, the air was still,
The stars were dead beyond the hill.
A lantern's glow, a fleeting spark,
Led wandering feet into the dark.

The house stood warped, its windows blind,
Its doors ajar, a trap aligned.
A voice called out, a velvet plea,
"Come closer, friend, and sit with me."

No face appeared, no form to see,
But whispers crawled from wall to tree.
A shiver crept through skin and bone,
For something breathed that was not known.

The chair rocked slow, though none sat near,
Its creak a song to conjure fear.
A knife lay bare on the oaken floor,
Its blade still wet with deeds of yore.

The scent of rust and earth was strong,
A graveyard hymn, a funeral song.
And from the shadows, long and thin,
A figure smiled with crimson skin.

Its hands were claws, its eyes abyss,
Its teeth promised a deadly kiss.
It pointed there, to the broken stair,
Where bodies hung like dolls in air.

"You're late," it rasped, with voice of dread,
"To join the dance of the forgotten dead."
A scream escaped but no one heard,
The walls consumed each muffled word.

And when they found the house at dawn,
The guest was gone, the chair rocked on.
But in the dust, fresh tracks remained,
A mark of death that can't be explained.

The Doll

A doll with a smile so wide,
Holds secrets no one can hide.
It laughs in the night,
With eyes full of fright,
As it waits by your bedside.

The Pendulum

A creak, a groan, a rope held tight,
It sways like a clock in the dead of night.
Each swing a promise, sharp and grim,
A judgment passed on life grown dim.

The shadows stretch, the floorboards sigh,
You beg for mercy, but mercy's shy.
Above, the beam gives one last moan,
And you are left to swing alone.

Supper's Elegy

The flesh is tender, marbled fine,
Each cut a work of grand design.
A hint of salt, a touch of spice,
Transforms the raw to something nice.

The texture yields beneath my blade,
A softness only time has made.
Sweet juices drip, a crimson flow,
The warmth within begins to glow.

I savour marrow, rich and deep,
Its taste a promise I will keep.
Each bite a story, bold, complete,
A symphony of life, replete.

But oh, the flavour none can feign—
The salt of tears, the tang of pain.
For every course, a soul must pay,
And mine? To feast the human way.

Footsteps in the Fog

The mist devours the cobbled street,
Where unseen steps and shadows meet.
A whisper trails; the air grows tight,
A phantom walks the edge of night.

The click of heels, the scrape of stone,
You glance behind, but you're alone.
Yet closer still, the rhythm drums,
Your breath betrays the fear that comes.

A scream is choked; the night won't tell,
Who stalks the fog—or where you fell.

Bloodstained Birds

A feather floats, a beak turns red,
A murder gathers overhead.
Their cries crescendo, sharp and shrill,
An omen perched upon the hill.

You turn away, but still they stare,
With patient eyes and vacant care.
They watch the flesh, they scent the sin,
And know the cracks beneath your skin.

When silence falls, their wings take flight,
And leave you bare to endless night.

The Watcher

Silent in the dark,
Eyes that burn, unblinking, cold—
Death moves through the night.

The Keyhole

Behind the door, a faint cliché—
The scuffle soft, the game they play.
But you, with eyes pressed to the lock,
Have seen too much for time to stop.

A hand extends, the shadow grows,
A blade reflects the room's tableau.
A gasp escapes, the lights go dim,
The watcher falls where none see him.

The door creaks open, slow, and wide—
And now, the keyhole peers inside.

The Murmur

In the quiet, past the grieving, in the hours most
deceiving,
Came a sound—low, soft, and fleeting—like a
pulse that kept repeating.
At my window, shadows lingered, clawing panes
with ghostly fingers,
And the voice, a breath unbroken, whispered
truths I'd left unspoken.

"Do you hear me?" murmured softly, tones both
tender, dark, and lofty.
"Do you feel the weight you carry, all your sins
that tarry, tarry?
Each misstep, each word unspoken, every vow
you've left as broken,
Feeds the hollow where I slumber; feeds the depths,
and pulls you under."

"Who are you?" I dared to question, though my
voice held no direction.
In the dark, the answer trembled, like a thing too

cursed, assembled.
"I am guilt you buried deeper, I am sorrow, liar,
reaper.
I am Murmur, ever seething—I am silence turned
to breathing."

Through the walls it wept and shivered, every
shadow stretched and quivered.
By my bed it crouched and waited, like a sentence
premeditated.
"Do you think your hands are cleaner, though
they scrubbed the stain unseen here?
Do you dream the past has faded, when the cost
remains unpaid yet?"

With a cry, I fled its calling, down the stairs and
through the sprawling
Rooms that once were lit with laughter, now
consumed by its hereafter.
Every mirror showed it clearer—eyes that burned,
a face drawn nearer,
And its breath, a venomed sermon: "Guilt is mine,
and you're my burden."

Still it followed, ever speaking, feeding off the fear
it's seeking.
"Shall we count the wrongs together? Shall we
name them, one forever?
Every thought you tried to smother, every wound
dealt to another—
I am here to weigh and measure, pain and guilt,
the final ledger."

Through the halls I ran unending, every corner
dark, descending.
Soon the walls began to narrow, caged within this
dreadful marrow.
"Stop," I begged it, barely breathing, though its
voice was still unsheathing.
"Stop," I whispered, shaking, crying, and it
laughed, so close, replying:

"Stop? You think there's peace in silence? Stop?
You think there's no reliance?
No escape exists, no freeing, when your guilt
becomes my being.
Do you think these walls will spare you? Do you

think the dark won't dare you?
Only one door holds salvation: death is guilt's
emancipation."

Weak and beaten, I stood heaving, all my hope a
dream deceiving.
At the window, open, waiting, stood the wind, its
call berating.
"Murmur," whispered through my senses, stealing
strength, erasing tenses.
"Jump," it sighed, its tone insistent. "End this
burden—go the distance."

And with trembling hands, I yielded, to the dark
my soul I fielded.
As the ground rose fast to meet me, still its voice
refused to free me.
"You are mine," it whispered, hollow. "I am
Murmur. I will follow."

A Flicker in the Dark

Candle burns so low.
The flame wavers; breath unseen.
You are not alone.

Clockwork Murder

The gears tick loud in the lonely shop,
A measured beat that will not stop.
The watchmaker smiles, his hands precise,
Each movement fine, a stroke of ice.

His patrons come, they always do,
To have their time reset anew.
But when they leave, the ticking fades,
For in their chests, his blade invades.

The clocks remain; they mark the deed,
A quiet end to mortal greed.

A Game of Shadows

The theatre flickers, the screen alive,

The killer's craft begins to thrive.

A scream erupts, but no one stirs,

They're trapped within the plot that purrs.

From velvet seats, the watchers freeze,

As shadows stretch with practised ease.

The silver glint, the final reel,

Reveals the truth they dared conceal.

And as the credits start to crawl,

The audience is dead to all.

Deadly Silence

No scream can pierce this vacant room,
No echo breaks the creeping gloom.
A ticking bomb, unseen, unheard,
Marks every breath with its cursed word.

You move too slow, the walls close in,
The silence wraps around your skin.
A snap, a crack, the time runs out,
And then... a whisper, soft as doubt.

The quiet holds what none can see—
A silent death, eternity.

The Unseen Creeper

The room's too quiet, the air too thin,
You feel it lurking, creeping in.
A scrape of stone, a fleeting sound,
Yet nothing moves upon the ground.

Its form grotesque, its face askew,
Its hunger sharp, its patience true.
A broken neck, a lifeless fall,
Is all it leaves—its silent call.

Don't trust the lights; they flicker faint.
No prayer can save, no holy saint.
Just keep your eyes and hold them wide,
Or join the others who have died.

The Curse

A curse was placed on this land,
The ghost of a man, cold and bland.
He stalks in the night,
A shadow of fright,
And whispers: "I'll take you by hand."

The Man in the Window

A shadow lingers in the pane,
Its shape both foreign, yet mundane.
You see it there, at dusk's descent,
A figure framed, a silhouette bent.

He watches you, his posture slight,
Through the amber glow of fading light.
You shut the blinds, but still you feel,
The presence there, the unseen zeal.

A knock resounds, the night grows thin,
Your pulse becomes a violin.
No steps approach, no shadows stray,
Yet something's near—it will not stay.

The door creaks wide; you gasp in fright,
The room is still, no man in sight.
But from the glass, his grin peers back,
Your final breath, his last attack.

Razor's Edge

There once was a barber so sly,
Who offered each cut with a lie.
"You'll look quite your best,"
He said with a jest,
As his blade kissed their throats goodbye.

The Silent Caller

The phone rang sharp at half past two,

Its voice too soft, its tone askew.

A whisper low, a name they said,

That chilled my bones and turned my head.

I glanced behind; no one was there,

But still, I felt a phantom stare.

The line went dead, the sound went flat,

Yet in the room, I smelled his hat.

The scent of rain, of leather worn,

A spectre dressed in shadow born.

And though I locked the door that night,

His knock returned, at morning light.

They Crawl Inside

Something stirs, beneath the flesh,
Poison spreads, the venom's mesh.
Inside, you feel the legs, they crawl,
Digging deeper, as shadows fall.
Every heartbeat screams in vain,
Resting, as they claim your pain.

The Hourglass

The sand descends, each grain a sigh,
A fleeting moment whispering: die.
The glass reflects a hollow gaze,
A life consumed by endless days.

The sands once slow now pour with speed,
Each pulse aligned to endless need.
The timepiece ticks, its cruel refrain,
A song that drills into the brain.

And as the final grains dissolve,
The pact you made begins to solve:
For what you asked, the price was steep—
Eternal debt, no time to sleep.

The hourglass shatters, your scream unspools,
A pawn forever in fate's dark tools.

unheard Cry

In the empty house,
A scream blooms, unheard, unseen.
Walls drink every word.

Cage of the Mind

A door that's locked, a room so bare,
The walls close in, the breath, the air.
The thoughts you keep, the ones you fear,
They turn to whispers, always near.

The cage is built inside your head,
A thousand voices left unsaid.
You try to scream, you try to flee,
But it's your mind that's holding thee.

The mirrors crack, the shadows creep,
The truths you buried rise from sleep.
There's nowhere left to hide from you,
No escape, no place to strew.

And when the walls begin to fall,
You'll realize it was you—after all.

One Step Behind

Footsteps echo close.

Yours—or another shadow's?

Don't stop. Never stop.

The Staircase

The staircase groans beneath my tread,
Each step a cry, a plea for dread.
The rails, they twist like serpents' spines,
While shadows climb in crooked lines.

The echo mocks my cautious pace,
Each hollow step a death's embrace.
Upward still, though silence calls,
A sudden thud—the whole world stalls.

I turn to see what wasn't there,
A figure shrouded, limbs of air.
It points ahead, to where I climb,
A warning toll of borrowed time.

At the top, a mirror stands alone,
Its surface cracked, its face unknown.
And there I see my final fate,
An empty shell, a step too late.

Silent Witness

The painting watched over the room,
Its eyes filled with secrets of doom.
The guests tried to laugh,
But none saw the gaffe—
The artist had sealed them in gloom.

The Lover's Knot

I tied the rope with trembling care,
A lover's knot for the stagnant air.
Its fibers whispered promises sweet,
Of a silence where despair might meet.

The chair stood firm, a solemn steed,
A silent witness to my need.
Its legs did creak, a mournful sigh,
As if to question: Why not try?

But try, I did—my final jest,
To slip the noose, to find my rest.
The world grew tight, my vision blurred,
A choking hymn, no savior heard.

Yet in the dark, as air grew thin,
I felt the walls begin to grin.
The shadows laughed, their fingers pried,
And whispered: Live? Or let us inside?

The knot did twist, the rope did bite,
Its hunger raw, its grip too tight.
But from my throat, no final plea,
Just hollow gasps in symmetry.

For death's a friend who does not speak,
A quiet wraith, both kind and bleak.
It holds you close, its kiss is cold,
But leaves you hanging—never bold.

And when they find me, swaying slow,
The chair below, the tale they'll know.
Yet on the rope, a stain of red—
Not from the neck, but tears I bled.

A lover's knot, a cruel design,
Bound not by death, but life's decline.
And in that room, where silence reigns,
The echo hums of tethered chains.

Cracked Mirror

A man stared into a glass,
And saw his reflection bypass.
His image, it grinned,
As the real him thinned,
And stepped through the cracks
en masse.

Nameless Depths

Beneath the waves, where light won't tread,
Where life twists forms the sane would dread,
A temple looms in brine and stone,
Its priests long-dead, their gods unknown.

The glyphs upon its walls confide,
A truth no mind could hope to bide.
For written there in viscous ink,
Are whispers that drive men to brink.

A pulse, a sound, the deep replies,
The beast below begins to rise.
A thousand limbs, each tipped with eyes,
Its scream a hymn to endless skies.

We fled the shore, but still it came,
Its name unspoken, yet the same.
For in my dreams, I hear it roar—
A nightmare bound forevermore.

Abyssal Call

Stars burn cold above.
The tide whispers secrets foul.
We drown in their gaze.

The Colour Beyond

They found it first in the barren clay,
A thing that shifted, writhing away.
Not colour as we have known or seen,
But something that slipped through realms
between.

It hummed, it pulsed, it drank the light,
It warped the day, it stained the night.
And those who touched its trembling core,
Were never quite themselves once more.

Their eyes would glint with a fevered gleam,
Their thoughts would twist, their minds unseam.
Until they whispered in tongues unknown,
And vanished beneath the spectral throne.

Still, the colour spreads, an endless glow,
A doom we birthed, we cannot know.

Hunger

Tentacles writhe high.

The sky fractures, stars dissolve.

We are devoured.

The Knife in the Curtain

The shower steamed; the world grew thin,
And masked within, the blade leaned in.
The curtain snapped; the scream was shrill,
A single stroke, the world went still.

But then the body rose once more,
Its eyes wide shut, its throat still sore.
The mirror cracked; a figure grinned,
The victim's death, a tale to spin.

For shadows lurk where dreams unwind,
And life is cruel, but death is blind.
Behind the walls, they always wait,
A killer's knife, a dreamer's fate.

Blade's Caress

Steel whispers to skin.
The final breath is silent,
Echoes in the dark.

Red Sky, Black Hands

The sunset bled like open veins,
The air alive with distant chains.
A field of bones stretched far and wide,
Where shadows move, though all have died.

A man stands tall, his fingers drip,
The crimson trail, his final script.
He hums a tune, his eyes askew,
His footsteps chase, though not by view.

No place to run, no place to hide,
The dream bends, warps, and opens wide.
And when you fall, he'll meet you there,
With glassy grin and vacant stare.

For even waking cannot save,
The hunted soul from this dark grave.

The Shunned Altar

A traveller lost in the mire,

Stumbled upon a dark spire.

Its stones breathed despair,

Its winds reeked of prayer,

And the gods beneath would

conspire.

Shape in the Shadows

The night is quiet, deathly still,
The air as sharp as winter's chill.
A shadow lingers by the fence,
Its outline blurred, its presence dense.

No breath, no sound, no mortal pace,
Yet there it waits, with hollow face.
You blink—it's gone, but in its stead,
The primal fear, the living dead.

A crunch of leaves, a distant tread,
A flash of steel where blood is shed.
The shape will come, it always will,
To take the life it means to kill.

No door can hold, no lock can bind,
A predator beyond the mind.
And as the clock strikes dead of night,
It steps from shadow into sight.

Claws in the Void

There once was a hand in the night,
Whose claws brought the children
such fright.
But when they awoke,
The hand did not joke—
It dragged them to endless twilight.

They Lurk Beyond

The static crackles, screens go black,
A distant voice, a low attack.
The signal fades, the power dies,
The stars dissolve in empty skies.

The world grows thin, the air runs cold,
As something stirs, relentless, bold.
Not men, not beasts, but things unmade,
With empty eyes and sharpened blade.

You see them there, just past the veil,
Their faces wrong, their bodies frail.
And when they come, it's far too late—
A march of death, a call to fate.

No gods to beg, no place to run,
No rising dawn, no morning sun.
For when they feast, their banquet grows,
The void devours all it knows.

Fogbound

The lighthouse is dim.
Figures walk where waves should churn.
Eyes glow through the mist.

The Mirror's Ghost

In the shadowed night, when time drips slow,
And dreams take shapes we barely know,
I sat alone in weary thought,
A prisoner of the calm I sought.
The clock hummed low, the air grew chill,
And silence pressed, oppressive, still.
Before me stood, as dark as sin,
A mirror broad, with silvered skin.

Its frame was carved in twisted vines,
And ghosts of stories traced its lines.
An antique thing, both stark and grim,
Its presence whispered something dim.
I gazed within, my face was bare,
Yet shadows seemed to linger there.
I leaned in close, against my sense,
And felt the pull, the darkness dense.

Sudden, sharp—a breath that froze—
The air around me sharply rose.
From the depths of glass, a shape unfurled,

A thing not bound to mortal world.
Eyes, hollow wells, of glinting pain,
A face half-formed, yet whole again.
Its voice, like winds through broken halls,
Spoke softly first, then screamed and called:

"Who stands before this wretched pane,
Who dares to speak my name in vain?
Your gaze has woken what should rest;
Now face the curse you have confessed."
I stepped back, heart a frantic drum,
Yet through the glass it still would come.
Its fingers clawed, its visage pale,
A mourning specter, lost, and frail.

"What do you want?" I stammered low,
But deep within, I had to know.
Its lips curled dark—a ghastly grin,
As if it pierced the guilt within.
"I want no coin, no plea, no plea,
I crave but one—your company.
For every mirror holds a door,
And some reflections bind us more."

The words it wove, like poisoned thread,
Chilled the marrow, filled with dread.
"My soul," it hissed, "was trapped by pride,
A slave to glass until I died.
Each mirror, then, a prison made,
To haunt the lives I once betrayed.
And now, my hand extends to thee,
To take your place, and set me free."

Its hands reached through, so thin, so cold,
A haunting pull, a grasp so bold.
I felt my breath begin to thin,
As though its touch drank all within.
"No!" I cried, and struck the frame,
But mirrors hold a deeper claim.
Its laughter rang, both deep and dry,
"None leave the mirror till they die!"

Then, with a burst of desperate will,
I grabbed the lamp and smashed until —
The glass was shards, the frame was split,
Yet still the ghost would not submit.
Its shape now loomed in broken air,

A shattered thing, beyond repair.
"You think this ends? Fool, mortal bound!
In every glass, I still am found."

I fled the room, my pulse a storm,
The chill of death a looming form.
And every window, every pane,
Reflected back its face again.
The mirrors screamed, the windows wailed,
The ghost pursued, unchained, unveiled.
Its voice, a hiss, a dreadful hymn:
"You broke the glass but freed me in!"

Now, years have passed, yet still I see,
The spectre's face, unyielding, free.
In every screen, in polished stone,
Its hollow eyes won't leave me alone.
The ghost, a shadow at my side,
Will haunt me 'til I too have died.
And thus I warn, with trembling breath:
Beware the mirrors—they may bring death.

The Keys to Hell

The door was locked for countless years,
Its iron bands held fast by fears.
The preacher's warnings, dark and grim:
"Don't turn the key; don't let them in."

But curious hands can't resist the touch,
The promise of secrets proved too much.

The lock gave way, the door swung wide,
And from within, the world had died.

A hiss of wind, a fetid breath,
The threshold marked by living death.
The dark poured out, alive, aware,
Its tendrils thick with tainted air.

Now shadows stalk the chapel walls,
Their voices echo through the halls.
The keys still dangle, slick with dread,
For what they turned will not be dead.

Man on the Hill

A man stood at the top of the hill,
His presence electric, his posture still.
No eyes in his face,
Yet he saw every place,
And he whispered: "You're part of the
kill."

The Endless Pursuit

It never runs, it never hides,
It only stalks, it only bides.
A patient hunter, sure and slow,
Its path is fixed, the death you know.

You flee through streets, through barren fields,
No locked door stops, no weapon shields.
Its footsteps echo in your mind,
No time to stop, no rest to find.

And when you think you've left its gaze,
It steps from shadows, eyes ablaze.
A force of death, a nameless fear,
It's always close—it's always near.

The sun may rise, the night may fade,
But you're the debt that must be paid.
No breath, no life, no silent prayer,
Can stop its march—it will be there.

Darkness Walks

In the alley, the darkness will hum,
A dirge for the weak and the numb.
It takes you away,
Where no light can stay,
And whispers: "Your time has come."

The Signal

The broadcast comes, a silent tone,
A frequency that chills the bone.
Its hum invades the fragile brain,
And leaves the mind forever stained.

You try to switch the dials away,
But static screams, the tones will stay.
Your thoughts dissolve, your heartbeats slow,
The signal feeds, it makes you grow.

No longer flesh, no longer free,
You join the swarm of what will be.
Machines that march, their hollow eyes,
A world consumed beneath gray skies.

And still it plays, that haunting sound,
A melody of lives unwound.

Fog's Embrace

Shapes move in the dark.
The fog whispers your last breath.
Cold hands pull you in.

The Watcher at the Window

The wind it howls, the trees bend low,
And still the face you do not know
Stares through the glass with hollow eyes,
A twisted gaze that never dies.

You've heard the whispers, light as air,
The way it lingers, always there.
A crack in time, a fleeting glance,
A shadow moves, the world's last dance.

At first, you think it's just your mind—
A trick, a fever, or just the grind
Of life, too tired, too worn, too deep—
But now, the watcher doesn't sleep.

Each night, it waits behind the glass,
And with the dawn, it turns to pass.
But once you see it, once it's real,
It's coming for you, it knows the deal.

You hear the door, the creak, the slam,
The footsteps drag, they're closing in.

And in the dark, the watcher grins,
For you're its prey; the hunt begins.

Falling Silence

Rope tightens, breath fades,
Shadows sway in quiet dance—
The final release.

The Demon's Throne

I wake, but not; my body's chained,
To a dreamless void, my soul constrained.
Eyes wide open, yet I can't see,
The world around dissolves from me.

A shadow stirs, it starts to grow,
From corners dark where nightmares flow.
A weight descends, a crushing stone,
Its hands cold flesh, my chest its throne.

It leans in close, its breath decayed,
A rancid fog where fears are made.
Its voice like shards, a cracking groan,
"Welcome back. You're never alone."

I see its shape, a twisted frame,
Its hollow eyes a burning flame.
The whispers twist, they scrape, they bite,
Each word a claw that steals my light.

I try to move, to scream, to fight,
But I'm a prisoner to the night.
My muscles locked, my voice won't rise,
The world is silent, except its lies.

"Why struggle now?" it purrs, amused,
"This is your place, your mind abused.
Each time you sleep, I'll drag you near,
To feast on every waking fear."

Its nails press deep, the pain is real,
A vivid horror I can't conceal.
I taste the blood, the panic spreads,
As laughter echoes in my head.

And then it fades, the weight is gone,
The demon slips into the dawn.
But even awake, its grip remains,
A haunting chill that scars my veins.

Tonight, I know it will return,
To watch me writhe, to make me burn.
For sleep is a gate, a cursed domain,
Where terror rules, and shadows reign.

The Midnight Caller

It's always at midnight, the phone will ring,
A sound that brings a certain sting.
The voice on the line, so low and dry,
Says, "I'm here now—don't ask why."

You try to speak, but it won't stop,
The voice, it climbs, it climbs to the top.
It calls your name, it calls your past,
And all your secrets, they've been cast.

You hang the phone, but it still rings,
A tortured sound that never clings.
You lock the door, you close the blinds,
But the voice is there inside your mind.

And in the dark, the silence speaks,
For you've been marked, your soul it seeks.
For the midnight caller comes at last,
To pull you down where shadows pass.

Crimson Dreams

Blades scrape on the walls.
Laughter sharpens every edge.
No escape from sleep.

Silent House

The house is quiet, every door closed,
But somewhere deep, the darkness grows.
In the walls, the whispers stir,
A tale of sorrow, a deadly blur.

The stairs creak soft, the floorboards bend,
A shadow waits, a voice to send.
A scream will echo, but none will hear,
The house has eyes, the house has fear.

It watches close, it waits for you,
For every step, it follows too.
The lights flicker, the doors slam shut,
And in the corner, something cuts.

The clock ticks loud, the hour draws near,
The house will take what it holds dear.
You try to leave, but it's too late,
The walls are closing, sealing fate.

Carnage's Cradle

Flesh tears apart with a sickening sound,
Blood paints the floor, soaking the ground.
The air smells of rot, of death, of doom,
The room is a crypt, a maddening tomb.

A blade gleams sharp, a hand so cold,
A smile forms, twisted and bold.
The victim's scream, a broken chord,
The agony, a sweet reward.

The walls are covered in red, in mess,
Each corner hides more to suppress.
A mask of death, an eerie face,
Chasing souls, a grim embrace.

There's no escape, no prayer, no plea,
Just darkness, and the cruel decree.
The carnage speaks in whispers vile—
Surrender now. It's been a while.

Reflection

The mirror cracks, the glass it weeps,
A reflection twisted, something creeps.
The face you see, it's not your own,
It smiles back, a truth unknown.

You turn away, but it's still there,
A hollow stare, a vacant glare.
Each time you blink, it moves more near,
A chilling voice you cannot hear.

The house is empty, yet it calls,
The halls are still, but something falls.
A shadow moves behind the door,
It waits for you, forever more.

You turn again, the room is cold,
The mirror lies, but it's been told—
There's nowhere left to run or hide,
The truth you see is not denied.

The Longest Goodbye

The rope was coarse, its fibres thick,
A silent promise, cruel and quick.
I tied the knot with shaking hands,
A grim resolve, no future plans.

The noose embraced my weary throat,
A sailor's knot, my final boat.
I stepped off into empty space,
To leave behind this cursed place.

But ropes, it seems, can sometimes lie—
It snapped, and let me live to die.
I fell, a heap of bone and skin,
The world refused to let me in.

My lungs still gasped, my heart still beat,
The dirt rose up to meet my feet.
I cursed the earth, I cursed the sky,
For granting me no wings to fly.

So to the heights, I turned my gaze,
To end the thread, to end the maze.

A rooftop's edge, a leap of faith,
To find the dark, the final wraith.

I spread my arms, a bird in flight,
To pierce the veil of endless night.
But gravity, a fickle friend,
Delivered not the peace I'd penned.

Instead, the landing broke my frame,
Left screaming pain, and burning shame.
The bones were shattered, nerves alight,
A prison made of flesh and fright.

Still breathing, still here—no escape,
No exit clean, no final shape.
The world denied my desperate plea,
A grim encore of agony.

So there I lay, a heap, undone,
A battered shell that couldn't run.
But then the blade, my old, dear muse,
Whispered softly: You still can choose.

With trembling hands, I held it tight,
Its edge a lover, cold and bright.

The veins lay bare, the crimson streams,
A lullaby of broken dreams.

The first cut deep, the second true,
Each one a gate I stumbled through.
The blood flowed thick, a velvet flood,
A masterpiece of mortal mud.

The pain dissolved, the dark crept near,
A quiet void, devoid of fear.
And as the light began to fade,
I smiled, at last, the price was paid.

No rope, no fall, no fleeting lies—
Just open veins, and lullabies.
The longest path, the cruelest way,
Had led me here, where shadows stay.

And though the journey's scars remain,
I've found my peace within the pain.

The Abandoned House

Dust on the windows,
The floorboards groan with each step—
Whispers fill the air.

Flesh Harvester

Chains rattle, the air is thick,
A figure lurks with fingers quick.
The hooks they gleam, the blades they shine,
The blood, it flows, it's by design.

The flesh is torn, the skin is peeled,
A sacrifice, the deal is sealed.
The whimpering fades, the cries they cease,
As bones are carved, and pain's release.

No mercy here, no help in sight,
Only the harvest, endless night.
The figure moves, its work is true,
For flesh must feed, and blood renew.

It does not stop, it does not care,
It waits for you, with hunger there.
The heart will pound, the soul will break—
In the darkness, you will wake.

Let The Games Begin

The mask is cold, the eyes are blind,
But in your head, the voice is kind.
"You're here to play, there's no escape,
The time has come to seal your fate."

A breath, a shudder, a gasp of air—
The chains around your wrist, so fair.
You fight to move, to scream, to run,
But nothing changes—this game's begun.

The walls move in, the clock ticks down,
A distant sound, a ringing crown.
You thought you'd win, you thought you'd flee,
But this game, it's never free.

The rules are set, the choice is made—
A twisted mind will never fade.
You fight, you fall, you reach for more,
But every step just closes doors.

Web

A spider spins its cruel web,
Its prey caught in the silky thread.
It waits for the bite,
A meal for the night,
Until its victim is dead.

The Mirror

You stand before a glass so clear,
But what you see is all but near.
The reflection's wrong, the face is cold,
A twisted grin, a life untold.

"Look at yourself," the voice demands,
"See who you are with bloodied hands.
Do you deserve to breathe tonight?
Or will you fall into the fight?"

The mirror cracks, the shards fall fast,
And in the dark, your fate is cast.
A choice is clear—yet made too late,
For in this room, there's no debate.

You think you've won, you think you're free,
But the mirror shows what you can't see.
You've played the game, you've made your mark,
And now you're lost in the dark.

Haunting in the Walls

The house stands silent, old and grey,
Its walls, they whisper night and day.
A hollow sigh, a creak, a moan,
In every corner, they're not alone.

The air is thick, the light turns dim,
As shadows dance on every whim.
A flicker here, a distant call—
It's never quiet, not at all.

Beneath the floor, beneath the stone,
A voice so cold, a breath unknown.
It knows your name, it knows your fear,
The thing that lingers, always near.

But who will listen, who will care?
When time's long gone, it's still right there.
The house it waits, the house it feeds—
On fear, on blood, on desperate needs.

Creeping Shadow

It moves in silence, like a dream,
A thing that's part of what you've seen.
It lingers close, it waits for night,
A thing that hides just out of sight.

The eyes that follow, the breath you hear,
A presence close, a voice unclear.
It doesn't speak, it doesn't shout—
But you know it's there, without a doubt.

It feeds on fear, it feeds on dread,
The thing that's real, though long thought dead.
And every time you look away,
It inches closer, come what may.

It whispers promises of fate,
Of things that haunt, of things that wait.
You never see it, but you know,
It follows close, it will not go.

The Endless Hall

Footsteps echo loud,
The hallway stretches for miles—
No end, only dread.

The Forgotten Place

The doors are locked, the lights are low,
The place you've found, you do not know.
A room, a house, a long-forgotten town—
The past is here, it pulls you down.

The floorboards creak, the stairs they moan,
A place once loved, now overthrown.
A shadow moves, it calls your name,
And in its grip, you're all the same.

It doesn't speak, it doesn't show,
The place you're trapped, you cannot go.
The past has lived, the past has died,
But in this place, there's nowhere to hide.

The doors are closed, the windows sealed,
The secrets here will never yield.
A place of dust, a place of fright,
Where time has lost its sense of light.

Wounds That Heal

A wound so deep, you cannot feel,
A scar that lies, a truth unreal.
It bleeds no blood, it whispers no sound,
But still, it marks, it keeps you bound.

You try to run, you try to flee,
But every step brings you to me.
A shadow born from things undone,
A nightmare formed, yet never won.

The wound is not in flesh, but mind,
A cut that never fades behind.
It grows with fear, it grows with dread,
The healing never comes, instead.

The scar will stay, the pain will grow,
A mark that follows where you go.
And in the end, it's all you'll find—
A wound that heals, but keeps you blind.

Dollmaker

The eyes so wide, the smile so fake,

The doll you hold, the hands that shake.

It whispers soft, it pulls you near,

A toy of terror, feeding fear.

It moves with grace, it speaks your name,

But when it smiles, you feel the flame.

It's made of wood, it's made of cloth,

But in the dark, it's more than thought.

A thousand stitches hold it tight,

But the doll knows more than wrong or right.

It waits, it listens, it knows your mind,

A little plaything, cruel, unkind.

And when the light begins to fade,

It's no longer just a toy you've made.

Unseen Hand

There once was a hand that would creep,
In your nightmares, it'd silently seep.
It grabbed from the air,
But when you'd turn to stare,
It'd vanish, and leave you to weep.

Fog

In a town wrapped in thick, choking fog,

The people were lost in the smog.

With each passing step,

The terror was kept,

As it swallowed the street like a log.

Silence

Silent,
Eyes that pierce deep,
Chilling with every glance,
Behind it lies a soul that screams—
Hiding.

The Thing Beneath

The thing that lurks beneath the floor,
Its fingers crawl, its shadows pour.
It waits in silence, biding time,
Until the bell begins to chime.

And then it moves, and then it calls,
A voice that echoes through the walls.
Its hunger sharp, its teeth, its grin—
A thing that's never known to win.

It waits for you, its breath so cold,
To bring you down, to take your soul.
For once it starts, it won't stop soon—
Until the dark has claimed the moon.

Storm

The thunder crashes,
The lightning lights the black sky—
Something walks outside.

Under the Moon's Hollow Gaze

The livestock stir, a restless sound,
Beneath the stars, on cursed ground.
A hush descends, the air grows tight,
Something prowls the edge of night.

A shadow moves, sleek and lean,
A fleeting shape, a thing unseen.
Eyes like embers, aglow with thirst,
A hunger ancient, primal, cursed.

The goats lie still, their bleats have ceased,
An offering made for the midnight feast.
Two wounds carved deep, red rivers flow,
The mark of what you'll never know.

Its breath is hot, a sulphur mist,
Its claws a whisper, a ghostly twist.
It leaves no prints, it makes no sound,
But fear takes root in the blood-soaked ground.

In tales they speak of things that creep,
That steal the warmth where creatures sleep.

It comes with dusk, it fades with dawn,
A phantom flicker, then it's gone.

Yet still the fields bear its trace,
A silent curse, a hollowed space.
Look to the woods, the hills, the trees,
And fear the rustle of the breeze.

For when the moon hangs low and stark,
Beware the terror that haunts the dark.

The Door

A knock at midnight,
A door that creaks, unanswered—
Who waits on the other side?

Endless Trees

Beneath the canopy so vast,

A haunting figure glides like glass.

Limbs of shadow, a timeless tread,

It walks among the silent dead.

No wind disturbs the branches high,

No stars remain within the sky.

Yet something whispers, soft and thin,

"Don't turn around—it's closing in."

You run, but paths all twist and fray,

The woods don't let you slip away.

For in these trees, it lays its claim,

A faceless shape, with none to name.

Strings of the Mind

It plays a tune you cannot hear,
A melody of whispered fear.
Each note it strikes with patient hand,
Until your thoughts are strands of sand.

A flicker here, a shadow there,
You feel it move through stagnant air.
Its arms stretch wide, its form surreal,
A puppet master, cold as steel.

You try to scream, but breath is gone,
The world dissolves; you linger on.
For once you see its faceless guise,
You live within its hollow eyes.

Don't Blink

Don't blink, don't dare, don't close your eyes,

For in that instant, something lies.

A fractured statue, cold as stone,

Yet in its stillness, it's not alone.

A fleeting shift, a whisper's scrape,

No time to run, no hope to escape.

Each blink a gamble, a fleeting toll,

It moves to claim your fragile soul.

Its grin is sharp, its stare too wide,

You'll feel its breath though it cannot stride.

For in the dark, where shadows cling,

A single blink gives life to wings.

The Sugar's Sting

In the darkness, they're handed out,
The treats, the sweets, the luring doubt.
Wrapped in paper, colored bright,
A gift to savor, a gift of fright.

Bite once, and feel the rush inside,
A sweetness rising with the tide.
But then it stings, it burns, it aches,
A deadly price, a twisted fate.

It crawls beneath your skin, it seeps,
Into your heart where terror keeps.
You try to scream, but none can hear,
The candy's curse is drawing near.

The Trick

The moonlight glows on eager feet,
My child's laugh, a sound so sweet.
A basket full of stolen treats,
From door to door, from street to street.

Their eyes alight with sugar dreams,
The world, so bright, or so it seems.
I watch them tear through wrappers thin,
Unaware of what's locked within.

A candy gleams, so soft, so bright,
A tempting gift in eerie light.
I can't protect them—too late, too soon—
My heart skips beats beneath the moon.

The first bite, a gleam of joy,
And then, my child begins to toy
With silence, stillness in their hands,
I hold their body, now unmanned.

Their lips go pale, their eyes grow wide,
I see the poison start to slide.

The sweetness turns to bitter death,
They gasp for air, a final breath.

I scream, I cry, but it's too late,
The sugar's bite, their twisted fate.
A mother's worst, a parent's plea—
To save a life that's fading free.

And as they slip through trembling hands,
I'm left with nothing but the sands.
The candy's curse, the trick, the lie—
I watch my child and hear them die.

The Shapeshifter's Cry

In the night, when shadows creep,

A figure stirs where secrets sleep.

A rustling sound, too close, too near,

A shifting shape, a primal fear.

Its eyes gleam bright, but not quite right,

A hollow gaze that steals the light.

It wears the skin of those it finds,

A twisted soul with human signs.

It howls beneath the moon's cold gaze,

A voice once loved, now lost in haze.

It knows your name, it knows your heart,

And from its prey, it'll never part.

A stolen laugh, a crooked grin,

The thing inside is wearing thin.

It calls your name, it mimics true,

But when you look, it's not you.

You hear the footfalls, soft and light,

But something's wrong beneath the night.

It knows your path, it knows your sound—
It wears the skin, it stalks the ground.

The wind grows cold, the air feels thick,
A creature circling, cruel and quick.
And if you flee, if you escape,
It'll follow with a twisted shape.

For when the skin is shed and worn,
The soul beneath is broken, torn.
And once it hunts, once it's begun,
It's never done until it's won.

Price of Blinking

A breathless moment, a fleeting stare,
It watches you—it's always there.
You think you're safe, you're sure it's so,
Until your eyes decide to close.

A brittle crack, a twisted grin,
The end begins where it begins.
No room for hope, no space for flight,
Just creeping death in endless night.

You hold its gaze, it holds your fate,
But every blink, it salivates.
The moment's near; you feel it come—
Your final blink, and then you're done.

Beneath the Surface

Her smile like a flower,
But beneath, the darkness grows—
Silken legs move fast,
In her web, I cannot flee—
I am hers to take at last.

Hollow Eyes

A crackling fire, a shadow's creep,
Around the hearth, the old ones speak.
"Beware the night, when dusk is near,
For something hunts, and it is here."

The wolf's cry calls, but twisted now,
A shape with human lips and brow.
Its eyes are hollow, black with spite,
The soul inside, a stolen light.

They say it wears the skin of kin,
To fool the heart and let it in.
But do not trust the voice you hear,
For once it speaks, you've drawn it near.

The old ones warn: don't turn to look,
Don't follow the call from the crooked brook.
For what you see is not what's real,
A skinwalker, hungry, made to steal.

Inside You

A little bite, a tiny sting,
The kind of thing you'd never think.
But now it moves beneath the skin,
A darkness, growing deep within.

You watch it crawl, a shadowed creep,
And try to wake from this dark sleep.
But each new hour brings more dread,
As something stirs beneath your head.

It burrows deep, it twists, it writhes,
A thousand legs beneath your sighs.
You claw at your skin, but nothing's there—
The spiders feed, the bite's despair.

Now it's too late, you cannot run,
The spiders feast beneath the sun.
And when they burst, you'll feel the dread—
A thousand deaths within your head.

The Presence

A figure in the dark,
Stairs stretch down, a hollow heart—
It watches, it waits.

Eyes in the Dark

There's something here, it's hard to see,
A flicker, a breath, a shadow's plea.
You feel it crawling, creeping close,
And every step you take, it grows.

A figure in the blackness stands,
No words, no sounds, no moving hands.
Just eyes that follow, dark as night,
That haunt you through your every fright.

It calls to you, it knows your name,
And all who descend are never the same.
The deeper you go, the less you breathe—
For in the dark, you'll never leave.

Stretching Depths

The stairs below you stretch on and on,
A thousand feet, yet none to dawn.
A breath that chills,
A presence that thrills,
And soon your light is gone.

Drowning

The water's grip, tight as steel,

Pulls me under, a fate I feel.

A world of silence, dark and cold,

No light to grasp, no hand to hold.

The surface fades, a distant dream,

As lungs burn with a stifled scream.

Every breath a fight for air,

But all that's there is a cold, wet snare.

The waves crash hard, no mercy found,

Each pull drags deeper, no solid ground.

A current strong, a force unseen,

It drags me down, relentless, mean.

The panic sets in, wild and fierce,

A primal fear, a final pierce.

Eyes wide open, but nothing to see,

Just endless dark and the drowning sea.

My chest tightens, the fight runs thin,
The water's edge too strong to win.
The thrashing slows, the struggle wanes,
As the body succumbs to water's chains.

The world above, it slips away,
A fading light, a distant day.
The water's grip, it holds me tight,
Pulling me into the endless night.

The last breath taken, filled with brine,
No longer mine, no longer fine.
In the depths, where the shadows roam,
I find my end, my final home.

The Silent Hunt

Lurking in the night,
A woman's form, so serene,
But with eyes that gleam.
Silk strands twist in deadly grace—
I feel her waiting in place.

Stairs

The steps descend, so quiet, slow,
A darkness calls from down below.
The air grows thick, a suffocating weight,
And every step leads to your fate.

You think you hear a whisper near,
A breath, a movement, feeding fear.
But look again—nothing's there,
Just endless stairs, and shadows, bare.

Each footfall echoes, loud and clear,
The sound of something drawing near.
But when you turn, there's nothing left,
Just emptiness where light has fled.

The air grows cold, your heart beats fast,
But there's no turning back, at last.
You're stuck, descending ever more,
With death waiting at the bottom's floor.

Crimson Ecstasy

In shadows deep where passion lies,
A twisted dance beneath dark skies.
Your touch, it burns, a fevered fire,
A lover's grip, both sweet and dire.

You whisper soft, a deadly charm,
As fingers trace along my arm.
With every stroke, my body shivers,
Your love, a blade that cuts and quivers.

Your eyes, they gleam, a haunting light,
As flesh is torn in the dead of night.
A scream, a sigh, they blend as one,
As pleasure and pain are deftly spun

Your hands, they carve with cruel delight,
A lover's kiss, both sharp and tight.
Each limb removed, a tender slice,
Your love, my death, the final price.

And as I break beneath your touch,
I find I'm craving you too much.

For in this horror, dark and sweet,
I'm lost within the pain's heartbeat.

You take me whole, then piece by piece,
A lover's torment, never cease.
In disarray, I find my end,
In your embrace, where death's a friend.

But in your eyes, a twisted grace,
I see my doom, a tender place.
For in this dance of death and lust,
Our love's a bond, both dark and just.

Final Embrace

In shadows cold, where cruelty reigns,
A ruthless dance on icy chains.
My touch, it chills, a bitter frost,
A merciless grip, the lines are crossed.

I speak in tones devoid of grace,
As I inflict the scars upon your face.
With every cut, your cries I savour,
Your pain a pleasure, a wicked flavour.

Your eyes, they plead, a feeble glare,
As I carve through the flesh laid bare.
A moan, a gasp, they fuel my pride,
As I delight in your slow demise.

My hands, they tear with no remorse,
A lover's rage, a brutal force.
Each wound inflicted with delight,
Your suffering, is my only rite.

And as you falter, broken, lost,
I revel in the tempest-tossed.
For in this torment, cold and clear,
I thrive on every drop of fear.

You're consumed, then left to bleed,
A vicious hunger I feed.
In chaos, I find my pleasure's grace,
In your despair, I carve my place.
For in this play of pain and scorn,
Our bond is darkly, coldly born.
In every scream and tear I see,
The joy of inflicting misery.

In the Shadows I Wait

I move through the dark where the streetlights
fade,
In the quiet corners, my plans are laid.
Each step is silent, my breath held tight,
The predator's patience, cloaked in night.

I've seen you before, I know your face,
Your every movement, your favorite place.
I've studied your paths, your routines so bare,
You walk unaware, while I linger there.

The thrill of the hunt ignites my mind,
In the shadowy spaces, I'm not confined.
Your laughter rings, a tempting sound,
But soon it will fade, with none around.

I follow you home, your steps are light,
You glance behind, but I'm out of sight.
A fleeting shadow, a rustling tree—
You'd never guess that it's only me.

Your door clicks shut, but locks won't keep,
The walls are thin, the house too cheap.
I linger outside, in the chilling air,
And dream of the terror we'll one day share.

The knife feels heavy, cool in my hand,
The final step in the game I've planned.
The world goes quiet, the time is near,
I feed on the taste of your budding fear.

The window cracks, the floorboards creak,
I feel your presence, the air grows weak.
You stir in your bed, a whispered sound,
But my footsteps vanish before they're found.

You wake, you scream, the terror pure,
Your heartbeat races, a panicked lure.
But it's too late; you're in my arms,
No escape now from my fatal charms.

The shadows swallow your final breath,
A dance of silence, a kiss of death.
And as the world forgets your name,
I move to the next, repeating the game.

Architect of Ruin

I see the world as threads to sever,
A tapestry frayed, beautiful, clever.
Each line I cut, a soul unwinds,
A masterpiece born from shattered minds.

Your breath, so sweet, it sings to me,
A melody ripe with fragility.
I don't just take—I mold, I shape,
Each scream a brushstroke, no escape.

I watch the fear bloom in your eyes,
The moment you see your fate arise.
Your struggles paint the floor in red,
A vivid hue where dreams have bled.

I hear your whispers, pleading cries,
The music of despair that never lies.
Each crack of bone, each gasp of pain,
A symphony that drives me insane.

But no, don't fear, I'm not done yet,
Your agony's art I won't forget.

I'll craft you into something new,
A gallery piece for none but few.

Your life was dull, a wasted thing,
But in my hands, you'll finally sing.
A perfect creation, a twisted muse,
Bound in the torment that I choose.

When I'm finished, the world will see,
The horror of what it means to be free.
For in my hands, the chaos grows,
And in your end, my genius shows.

So scream, so writhe, it's all for you,
This is the gift I'm meant to do.
No need to thank me, there's no reprise—
I live to destroy what others prize.

The Final Whisper

You've journeyed far through ink and dread,
Through crimson lines the lost have bled.
Yet now, dear reader, the time has come—
The last refrain, the final drum.

The air grows cold; the page feels thin,
The shadows crawl, they close you in.
A presence stirs beyond the veil,
Its breath a hymn, its voice a wail.

You thought these words were safe to read,
But now they root, they plant their seed.
The ink you touched, it stains your skin,
A pact was made—unknowingly within.

Each word you spoke within your mind,
Was heard by things you'll never find.
They wait in cracks where light can't creep,
And whisper truths that steal your sleep.

A tap-tap-tap upon the pane,
A shuffling sound you can't explain.

The book you clutch begins to hum,
A dirge of doom—your end has come.

The walls grow thin; the room distorts,
The world dissolves to blackened ports.
And from the dark, a figure crawls,
Its limbs too long, its body sprawls.

Its eyes, like coals, burn deep and bright,
Its jagged grin consumes the light.
It knows your name; it knows your fear,
It's always been so very near.

You try to scream, but words won't form,
The air grows thick, a raging storm.
The book snaps shut, yet still it sings,
A spell unleashed, a curse it brings.

And as you run, its voice will trail,
A ghastly laugh, a mournful wail.
For once you've read this cursed refrain,
You'll never be the same again.

So close the book, but know this truth:
Its mark will haunt your fleeting youth.

For stories end, but not the dread—
The final whisper lives… **inside your head.**

A Final Omen (For the Fools Who Reached the End)

Well, look at you. You made it to the end. Or did the end make it to you? Either way, congratulations—or condolences—seem in order. You've devoured the words, bled through the pages, and survived the shadows. But here's the thing about surviving: it's a temporary condition.

The book is finished, but the story isn't. Not really. You see, the moment you turned the last page, you invited something... lingering. Maybe it's just a shiver down your spine, a faint rustle in the corner of your room, or the whisper of your name in the dead of night. Ignore it if you like. That always works out well in the stories, doesn't it?

Oh, and don't think you can hide this book away on a dusty shelf or toss it into a fire. It's not the book you need to fear anymore—it's what it's left behind in *you*. Those words you read, the ones that gnawed at your mind and curled into the cracks of your soul? They're still there, feeding, growing, waiting.

Perhaps tonight, when you close your eyes, you'll feel the weight of their gaze. Or maybe it'll be tomorrow, when you catch your reflection moving just a second too late. Time is patient, and so are they.

So go ahead, shut the cover. Walk away. Convince yourself it's just a book. Just paper and ink. But when the silence grows too loud, when the dark feels just a little too deep—remember this: you finished the book, but something else might just be getting started.

Sweet dreams. If you're lucky enough to have them.

With eternal malice,
The Author

About the Author

K.W. Krieger was not born—he emerged, fully formed, from the darkest recesses of a crumbling library where Edgar Allan Poe's whispers mingled with the distant screams of Lovecraftian nightmares. Raised on the grim theatrics of Shakespearean tragedy, their formative years were spent dissecting the macabre beauty of sonnets, soliloquies, and Satanic verses.

An unapologetic devotee of the weird, the grim, and the grotesque, Krieger draws inspiration from blood-stained cinema screens and the fever dreams of horror masters. From the creeping dread of *The Exorcist* to the flesh-bound chaos of *Hellraiser*, from the psychological labyrinth of *The Shining* to the viscera-splattered terror of *Hereditary*, they've marinated their mind in nightmares, gore, and the art of unsettling audiences.

When not conjuring haunted verses, Krieger spends their nights sipping black coffee strong enough to show up on a drug test and writing in the eerie glow of flickering candles that occasionally blow themselves out. Their workspace is a shrine to chaos: battered typewriters, ink-stained journals, and a collection of curiosities that would make a witch's lair look quaint. There are whispers that Krieger's Favorite writing companion is a mirror that sometimes reflects things that shouldn't be there.

Known to wander abandoned places and graveyards for "research," Krieger believes that darkness isn't just a part of life—it's the part that makes it worth exploring. They collect nightmares the way others collect stamps, and their dedication to the macabre ensures every story they pen drips with dread, despair, and just the right amount of terror to make you sleep with the lights on.

Their work is fuelled by the philosophy that fear is art, and every scream is a symphony. They humbly (or not so humbly) dedicate their writing to the masters of terror who came before, the devils who lurk in every shadow, and the restless spirits who visit at 3:33 a.m.

Follow K.W. Krieger if you dare—though they cannot promise you'll like where they lead, and they guarantee you won't return unchanged.

Follow K.W. Krieger if you dare—though they cannot promise you'll like where they lead, and they guarantee you won't return unchanged.